Pioneer Church

Carolyn Otto

ILLUSTRATED BY Megan Lloyd

Henry Holt and Company / NEW YORK

AUTHOR'S NOTE

*T*HE STORY of the little church in Elisabethville is based on the history of Old Zion, a landmark building in Brickerville, Pennsylvania. Though the native Tuscarora had long hunted in the wilderness valley, and sometimes camped there, the first permanent settlers were from Germany. Like many European colonists, they came to America in search of richer farmland and better lives, and because they could worship as they wished.

Early services were held outdoors; homes were used in the winter. A log church had been built by 1735. In 1748 a new building was erected on the same site. The names of Peter Becker, Wendel Laber, and Jacob Keagy appear in church records at this time. The brick building of 1813 is the Old Zion of today, incorporated as a historic landmark in 1960. Among the ministers who served there were Christian Weiler, W. T. Gerhard, and George B. Raezer. The other names are fictitious.

While this book is grounded in fact, parts of the story are fiction. History may not reveal the whole, and records leave things out. Women and children are mentioned rarely, but their influence on the development of community and country cannot be denied. And although there's no specific tale of a mercenary soldier who married a nurse called Katarina, it is estimated that fewer than half of the Hessian survivors returned to Germany after the Revolution. Many Hessian soldiers had deserted to the Continental Army; many settled in America. Thus the new nation grew, and continued to grow.

All of that is history. It happened. So our story might have happened this way.

Henry Holt and Company, Inc. , *Publishers since 1866*, 115 West 18th Street, New York, New York 10011. Henry Holt is a registered trademark of Henry Holt and Company, Inc.

Text copyright © 1999 by Carolyn Otto. Illustrations copyright © 1999 by Megan Lloyd-Thompson. All rights reserved.

Published in Canada by Fitzhenry & Whiteside Ltd., 195 Allstate Parkway, Markham, Ontario L3R 4T8.

Library of Congress Cataloging-in-Publication Data

Otto, Carolyn. Pioneer church / by Carolyn Otto; illustrated by Megan Lloyd-Thompson. Summary: In the mid-1700s, four families build a log church on a hill in central Pennsylvania, and congregations worship in it and its replacement up through World War II. Based on the history of Old Zion Church in Brickerville, Pennsylvania.

[1. Church buildings—Fiction. 2. Pennsylvania—History—Fiction.] I. Lloyd-Thompson, Megan, ill. II. Title. PZ7.08794Fi 1995 [E]—dc20 95-42007

ISBN 0-8050-2554-5 / First edition—1999 / Designed by Martha Rago

The artist used oil paints on Belgian linen and pen, ink and watercolor on Arches paper to create the illustrations for this book.

Printed in the United States of America on acid-free paper. ∞

1 3 5 7 9 10 8 6 4 2

To my grandfather's grandfather Sam, who helped build a church in Fredonia, Kansas;

to my great-grandmother Belle, who played the organ there; and to my dad,

the Reverend Doctor Otto, who helped me keep history straight

—C. B. O.

To the Lloyds and Thompsons, the Hugheses, Schrefflers, and Campbells,

the Stones, Yorks, and Lightners, and others further back;

with special thanks to Peter Deen for introducing me to Old Zion

—M. L.

ONG BEFORE these houses were here, before the stores were built, back before anyone had even dreamed of the gas stations on either side of the street . . .

. . . Zachary Lapp, Jacob Keagy, Wendel Laber, and Peter Becker built a church on this hill.

Elisabeth Lapp and the other women took care of morning chores. Dishes were washed, floors scrubbed, rugs taken out for a shaking. Children scattered dried corn and stale bread for the chickens, for the ducks and the fat gray geese.

At noon Elisabeth tucked up her skirts and climbed the rough path to the building site. She carried two lunch pails, one in each hand.

The men had shoveled and smoothed the ground in a clearing on top of the hill. The church was by then a limestone foundation with walls that were three logs high.

They worked from dawn until dusk, sunrise to red sunset, from one day into the next. On the darkening afternoon of the sixth day, Zachary halloed down in answer to the dinner bell. Everyone would have to come up. There was something to see.

Elisabeth folded a collection of bowls and tin spoons into her best tablecloth, along with candles and a blue saltcellar. She ladled hot stew into a pot with wire handles. Loaves of bread were packed into baskets. The children were given packets of cheese or butter to carry, and jars of sweet pickles or compotes. Young Samuel led off with the lantern.

They found the men sitting inside the small church, hats in their hands and the work finally done.

Jacob Keagy, the Labers, Beckers, and the Lapps ate their supper by candlelight. The church smelled of stew and warm bread and freshly hewn wood. Outside, a great horned owl swept through the clearing, and a whippoorwill sounded three clear notes of song.

At first the four families worshiped alone, taking turns to read the lessons. Then another family settled in the valley, another family, and another.

Every Sunday more people came to the church on the hill. A visiting minister began to stop by on a regular basis—once a month in warm weather, and once in a while during cold spells.

He was there when Nathan Becker was christened, Samuel Laber was married, and Elisabeth Lapp was buried in the quiet churchyard.

On weekdays the church was used as a school for the children, for quilting bees and social dinners, and as a meeting place to talk about crops and taxes and roads.

Nearly everyone turned out for Zachary's birthday. It seemed lucky to celebrate a man's seventy-fifth year of life in 1775. That evening they decided to name the community in the valley. The vote was unanimous, honoring Zachary's suggestion that it be named after his wife. From then on, the settlement was called Elisabethville.

In just a few months, the townspeople would gather again . . . this time to discuss the Declaration of Independence and the coming war.

After the Battle of Brandywine, in 1777, the church became a temporary hospital. Rebecca Lapp and Katarina Vetter nursed the sick men, the hungry, the hurt. Among them were two soldiers fighting on the side of the British. They were Hessian mercenaries from Germany, lost and very frightened. Katarina spoke to them in German, dressed their wounds, gave them soup and brown bread. She took away their uniforms and burned them in secret, just beyond the silent gates of the churchyard.

One of the Hessian soldiers went off to fight with General George Washington. The other, Wilhelm Brubaker, stayed behind to marry Katarina Vetter. The wedding took place on a soft summer morning, and the church was so crowded that many people stood outside to listen through the open doors and windows.

The church was small, and Elisabethville was getting big. A new church was built in the valley. Not long after, a foundation was laid for another church, and its tall spire crept slowly into the sky.

One night the old log church caught fire. Women and children formed a bucket brigade, while the men shoveled a trench around the churchyard and prayed the flames wouldn't spread. By the time two horse-drawn fire engines had galloped up from Elisabethville, the church was past saving.

The next morning a small congregation gathered to look at the ruin, to mourn the little church, and to vote. They elected to build a new church on the same site, a church of brick and yellow pine, with a gray slate roof. They also named a full-time minister: Ezra Brubaker, son of Wilhelm and Katarina.

The new First Church of Elisabethville was dedicated in 1813. It had a coal-burning stove, an organ, and a fancy kerosene chandelier. A balcony was built high above the sanctuary, and arched windows patterned the floorboards with sunlight.

On cold Sundays, Ezra could hear the hiss of burning coal and the crisp jingle of harnesses outside. The congregation bundled into the pews, coats and cloaks and heavy wool wraps crowding everyone close together.

On hot days, the women waved paper fans. Lazy flies circled the sanctuary, and the horses switched their tails in the cool shade fringing the churchyard.

When Ezra Brubaker grew old and retired, other ministers took his place: Christian Weiler during the early years of the church, and the Reverend W. T. Gerhard through the Civil War. Men and women began to sit together for services, and women often read the lessons. The sermon was no longer given in German. The world was changing fast.

Rev. Weiler

The Reverend Gerhard and wife

George B. Raezer was called to the pulpit in 1912, the same year a horseless carriage first rolled into town. He led the congregation through the hard times of World War I, and then through World War II. When he retired in 1947, his parishioners decided to move to a new building—one that had electricity and city water, and a parking lot out back.

The First Church of Elisabethville was closed.

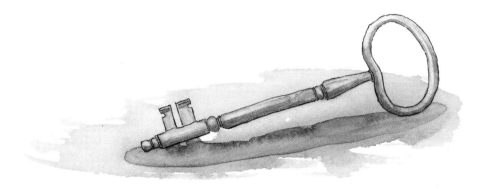

A pair of swallows built a nest on the iron branches of the kerosene chandelier. On windless nights an owl circled over the sagging roof and listened for the rustle and squeak of a tiny congregation of mice.

Many years passed before human voices came again to the sanctuary. One day, all at once, the church was filled with people working—cleaning, sweeping, patching and painting, knocking deserted nests from the balcony, from the pulpit and chandelier.

The First Church of Elisabethville is now a historic landmark.

As in other places across America, a part of history has been preserved. Yet history goes on, history grows, new stories resound within these walls. There are weddings held here, special events, festivals, and Christmas programs.

And every Easter Sunday, families park their cars along the dark streets below, and climb up to celebrate a sunrise service in the pioneer church on top of the hill.